E
Bi

Biro, Val

Gumdrop and the
steamroller

DATE DUE

9/15			

Gumdrop
and the steamroller

Val Biro

CHILDRENS PRESS, CHICAGO

This Gumdrop book has been especially
drawn, and written in simple words
and sentences, for *Stepping Stones*.
Val Biro's many other Gumdrop stories
are available as full-size picture books.

Library of Congress Cataloging in Publication Data

Biro, Val, 1921-
  Gumdrop and the steamroller.

  (Stepping Stones)
  SUMMARY: Gumdrop, Mr. Oldcastle's smart old car,
has a near-calamity with a steamroller.
  [1. Automobiles—Fiction] I. Title.
PZ7.B5233Gtb   [E]   76-50025
ISBN 0-516-03597-5

American edition published 1977 by
Regensteiner Publishing Enterprises, Inc.
All rights reserved. Printed in the U.S.A.
Published simultaneously in Canada.

Copyright ©1976 Val Biro
First published 1976 by Knight books and
Hodder & Stoughton Children's Books, Salisbury Road, Leicester

Gumdrop is a smart old car with
a black top. Mr. Oldcastle was driving
him along one day. They were going
home for lunch.

Round a bend, they had a shock! The
road was blocked by Jack the steamroller
and his driver Jock.

So <u>Gumdrop</u> had to stop. "Honk-honk"
went his horn.

But Jock the driver did not
hear. He thought the road
behind was clear.

5

Oh dear! With a "toot!" and a blow,
back came Jack, clackety-clack.

"Oh! Mind my car!" shouted Mr.
Oldcastle. "You are too near! Can't you
hear?"

"This is rum, by gum!" said the workmen who flocked to where the road was blocked.

Mr. Oldcastle did not want Gumdrop
knocked. So he looked back as he drove
backwards too. He had to mind the road
behind.

He had to look forwards too. There
was Jack, coming back, clackety-clack.
"Really," said Mr. Oldcastle, "this is
most unkind!"

The workmen began to shout and run about.

"Don't knock that car!" they shouted to Jock. But he did not hear and he did not look back.

Back came the steamroller, clackety-clack.

Mr. Oldcastle looked at Jack.

"Mind your back!" shouted the workmen, "look behind!"

Too late. With a whack and a smack, Gumdrop fell back and dropped into a ditch! With a "honk!" he went "ackety-ack" and stopped.

13

Driver Jock heard the smack and the whack and with a "toot" and a blow he stopped Jack too.

"Oh dear!" he said,
"I did not hear.
But never fear,
we will pull you clear!"

So Jock and the workmen started to pull.

But Gumdrop was far too heavy a car, and the ditch was as sticky and tacky as tar.

The road was smeary and the workmen all slipped and fell back with a smack!

"What a flop!" said the workmen to
Jock. "Gumdrop is stuck in the muck.
There isn't a hope."

18

"Don't sit and mope," said Jock. "Look, here is a rope. Jack will tow Gumdrop to the top."

So with a "toot"
and a blow, Jack
began to tow.
Clackety-clack!
    With a "honk"
Gumdrop came
slowly up from
below.

"Hurray!" said the workmen.
    "That's it! You're on your way."

"Thank you so much," said Mr. Oldcastle. "As for me, I am ready for my lunch. And you must ALL come back with me!"

So they all had a fine lunch.
And after all that honking and tooting
and blocking and knocking
and backing and smacking
and towing and blowing
by Gum! how they enjoyed it!
Yum-yum!